Timmy's Hiccup Cure

EGMONT

First Published in Great Britain in 2010
by Egmont UK Limited
239 Kensington High Street, London W8 6SA

Series created and produced by Jackie Cockle
Based on a script by Pete Reeves

Printed in China

The sun was shining brightly
through the Nursery window.

The little animals were unusually quiet.
They were sitting in a circle on the
classroom floor - it was reading time!

Osbourne watched over the animals as they
silently read their books. Otus was sitting beside
Ruffy, they were both concentrating very hard.

Ruffy was enjoying his book so much that
when he had finished, he went back to the
start and read it again!

Timmy was sitting beside Kid. He was reading his favourite book – it was about **FOOTBALL!**

Timmy waggled his ears in excitement as he turned the pages.

Suddenly, the silence was broken by a munching sound. Timmy turned around to see Kid had taken a large bite out of the corner of his book! He chewed loudly and with a large **GULP**, he swallowed the pages of his book.

Timmy could not believe what he was seeing!

Kid's chewing was disturbing Timmy, who
had been quietly enjoying reading his book!

Timmy turned around to look at Kid, who was still
chewing on the pages of his book.

Kid looked up at Timmy. He gave a little cough,
then with a little jump he made a funny noise.
HICCUP! HICCUP!

All the little animals stared at Kid,
as he jumped again.

RUFF!
Cried Ruffy, giggling at Kid.

Soon the cuckoo popped out of
the clock, it was break time!
Everyone was lined up to collect
their snacks from Osbourne.

Timmy was first in the queue, he collected
his snack bag. He was curious about what
might be making Kid jump.

Kid collected his snack bag.
HICCUP! HICCUP!

Osbourne showed Kid how to take
deep breaths to try and get rid of his hiccups.
Kid copied Osbourne, taking some deep breaths.

Timmy and Kid went through the gate
into the playground. Suddenly, Kid jumped.

HICCUP! HICCUP!

Timmy giggled, Kid's hiccups had not gone
after all. Kid was upset, his ears flopped as
he sat down on a tree stump and jumped.

Timmy sat down beside Kid, who gave another
little jump as he tried to eat some fruit.
Timmy tried feeding Kid. He prised his mouth
open and popped in some food, but still
Kid jumped.

Timmy really wanted to help his friend.

He tapped his little hooves, he wondered
how he could stop Kid from jumping.
Timmy thought very hard.

Timmy had an idea! He crept behind
Kid and took a really, really deep breath . . .

BAAAAAAAAAHHHHH!

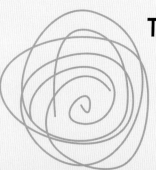

Timmy bellowed very loudly in Kid's ear.
Kid jumped and **HICCUPPED**
loudly back.

Timmy walked over to Kid and lifted his ear looking inside it and waggling it around.

BAAH!

Timmy had had another idea. He stood in front of Kid and waggled his own ears.

Kid copied and waggled his ears.

Soon both of the little animals were waggling their ears, until Kid jumped - **HICCUP!**

Timmy's plan hadn't worked, Kid was still jumping!

Timmy had another idea. Perhaps if Timmy jumped, then Kid would stop hiccupping! Kid watched in amazement as Timmy bounced and bounced and bounced!

Soon, Kid started bouncing too and they bounced right out of the courtyard gates until both exhausted, they sat down for a break.

Timmy was excited. He had cured Kid's hiccups!

Kid jumped, **HICCUP!**

As Kid and Timmy took a rest, they heard some loud **OINKS** and **HICCOS** from the playground.

Paxton and Apricot were having fun on the seesaw and Otus was twirling on the roundabout.

Timmy ran into the playground, with Kid bouncing and hiccupping behind him!

Timmy ran over to the seesaw.

OINK! OINK!

Paxton cried in excitement,
as Apricot let out a little **HICCO!**

Kid followed excitedly.
HICCUP! HICCUP!

Apricot rolled herself into a ball, rolling right
off the end of the seesaw.

BAAH! BAAH!

Timmy and Kid clambered
onto the high end of the seesaw.

Timmy and Kid started seesawing,
high up in the air.

Timmy was so excited he had forgotten
all about Kid's hiccups.

Kid was clinging tightly, **HICCUP!**
Kid flew high in the air.

BAAH! BAAH!

Timmy bleated, disappointed that Kid **STILL**
had the hiccups. He thought the seesawing
might have made them go away.

Timmy jumped down from the seesaw. Kid was still bouncing up and down, with Paxton on the other end of the seesaw. Kid was hiccupping loudly.

OINK! OINK!

Paxton was much heavier than Kid, so Kid was spending a lot of time high up in the air.

HICCUP! HICCUP!

Kid's hiccups were still making him jump!

Timmy thought hard. There must be a way to stop Kid's hiccups.

BAAH! BAAH!

He sat down and picked up his snack bag and searched inside. There was nothing inside.

BAAH! BAAH!

Timmy's ears drooped, he was so disappointed he couldn't help his friend. He really wanted Kid to stop jumping!

Yabba and Ruffy were playing with a beach ball.
They were playing catch, throwing it
back and forth to each other.

Ruffy was bored with the game
of catch. When Yabba passed the
ball to Ruffy, he kicked it hard.

QUACK! QUACK!

Yabba watched the ball sail right over her
head! The ball flew past her and landed
just beside Timmy. Meanwhile Kid was still
on the seesaw, bouncing up and down.

Without thinking, Timmy half-heartedly kicked the ball. The ball rolled and landed just under the seesaw.

Suddenly, there was a loud **POP!** Paxton had landed on the ball, which had burst.

BAAH! BAAH!

Timmy realised that the startled Kid was no longer jumping and his hiccups had magically disappeared!

Kid jumped down from the seesaw and hugged his friend. Finally, Timmy had found a cure for Kid's hiccups, even if it was an accident!